MYSTERY AT THE PARK

By Erin Soderberg
Illustrated by Duendes del Sur

ABDOPUBLISHING.COM

Reinforced library bound edition published in 2017 by Spotlight, a division of ABDO. PO Box 398166, Minneapolis, Minnesota 55439. Spotlight produces high-quality reinforced library bound editions for schools and libraries. Published by agreement with Warner Bros. Entertainment Inc.

Printed in the United States of America, North Mankato, Minnesota.
012016   092016

THIS BOOK CONTAINS
RECYCLED MATERIALS

PUBLISHER'S CATALOGING IN PUBLICATION DATA

Names: Soderberg, Erin, author. | Duendes del Sur, illustrator.
Title: Scooby-Doo and the mystery at the park / by Erin Soderberg ; illustrated by Duendes del Sur.
Description: Minneapolis, MN : Spotlight, [2017] | Series: Scooby-Doo early reading adventures
Summary: Scooby and the gang are helping out Lakeside Elementary School with sports day. But when the wagon that contains all the balls for the softball game mysteriously disappears, it's up to the gang to uncover the mystery and save the day.
Identifiers: LCCN 2016930650 | ISBN 9781614794691 (lib. bdg.)
Subjects: LCSH: Scooby-Doo (Fictitious character)--Juvenile fiction. | Dogs--Juvenile fiction. | Schools--Juvenile fiction. | Parks--Juvenile fiction. | Sports--Juvenile fiction. | Mystery and detective stories--Juvenile fiction. | Adventure and adventurers--Juvenile fiction.
Classification: DDC [Fic]--dc23
LC record available at http://lccn.loc.gov/2016930650

Spotlight
A Division of ABDO
abdopublishing.com

Scooby and his friends were at the park.

Scooby was excited to help their friend Mrs. O'Brien with Lakeside Elementary School sports day.

Daphne, Fred and Velma were in charge of the tug-of-war.

Shaggy and Scooby were going to help with snacks.

"Oh no!" cried Mrs. O'Brien. "The wagon with all the balls for the big softball game is missing! It was right here," she pointed.

Scooby tried to find the wagon, but all he found were footprints and kids running relays.

"Like, I hope a monster didn't take the wagon full of balls," said Shaggy.

"We better look for clues, gang," Fred said.

Scooby started to sniff around,
looking for the wagon and balls.
He hoped he wouldn't find a
monster.

Scooby looked under a table.
He found a family of ants
carrying their Swiss cheese
and crackers!

"Rum rum!" he licked his lips.
But he did not find the wagon
and balls.

Scooby found Shaggy by the ice cream cart.

"Hey, Scooby, did you find the wagon and balls?" Shaggy asked.

Scooby shook his head.

The sun was very hot.

"Like, we better eat this before it melts," said Shaggy.

"Rokay!" Scooby said.

Scooby and Shaggy found a
bag of potato chips next to the
swing set.
But no wagon and no balls.
And no monster.
They followed a butterfly down
the hill.

Velma, Fred and Daphne came across some kids from Mrs. O'Brien's class.

"Did you find the wagon?" a boy asked.

"We really want to play softball!" said a girl.

"Let's keep looking, gang," Fred told Daphne and Velma.

They passed a boy flying a kite.
"Have you seen a wagon filled
with balls?" Daphne asked him.
"Yes, I saw a wagon at the top
of the hill this morning," the
boy said.
"Let's check the hill for clues,"
Velma said.

Daphne, Fred and Velma ran to the top of the hill.

They found Shaggy on the grass taking a nap while Scooby sniffed around.

But there was no wagon full of balls anywhere.

"I don't understand," said Fred. "How can a wagon just disappear?"

Mrs. O'Brien saw Scooby and the gang and came over. "Any luck?" she asked.

"Ruh-roh!" Scooby pointed at some tracks in the dirt.

"Like, I hope those aren't from the monster!" Shaggy cried.

"Look," said Fred. "The tracks lead down the hill to the lake."

"Scooby, will you look in the lake
if I give you a Scooby-Snack?"
Daphne asked.

"Rokay!" Scooby said.

Scooby put on his scuba mask and
flippers.

He dove into the lake.

Scooby found the wagon full of balls at the bottom of the lake. "The wagon must have rolled down the hill and into the lake," Velma said.

"There was no monster," said Fred.

"You saved sports day, Scooby!" Mrs. O'Brien said.

"Scooby-Dooby-Doo!" Scooby barked.

The End